MW00938277

Little Pond Stories:
A Visitor

By Shennen Flannery

AcuteByDesign Publishing
Executive Publisher: Michele Sharpe-Thomas
ISBN: 978-1-943515-35-6

Fonts used: Harrington and Minion Pro

Illustrations and design by Ken Forgue
Interior layout by Meg Petrillo

AcuteByDesign
the little book company that could
A Michael Marion Sharpe Company

Little Pond Stories: A Visitor

In a land not far from here sits a beautiful place called Little Pond. It is not big like the ocean, or small like a puddle. Little Pond is a place where animals live all year long. There are fish, and birds, and bugs. There are frogs, and toads, and bats. Day and night, Little Pond is a busy place.

In the summer, butterflies roam from flower to flower, while the honey and bumble bees chase each other over red and white clover. Turtles rest on rocks in the sunshine, and birds sing songs in the trees. Until Mr. and Mrs. Beaver built their dam of mud, sticks, and stones, Little Pond was not a pond at all, but a zigzagged brook. Their house, called a lodge, grows larger every year. It is in the middle of the pond where Lady Canada Goose sits on her spring eggs until they hatch. The animals enjoy Little Pond thanks to Mr. and Mrs. Beaver. Without the dam, fish, turtles, frogs, and waterfowl would vanish. And without Mr. and Mrs. Beaver, Little Pond would return to a sad brook.

One lovely summer day, a new animal appeared. She was not large like an elephant, or small like a snail. In fact, she was unlike any animal. This visitor at Little Pond was human, and she moved quickly! Daisy Eloise Brown slid down an entire wet bank of  long grass as she ran to see Little Pond for the first time in her life, carrying an old map in one hand, and a Science book in the other. Both she threw into the air as she flew into the water, feet first, nearly hitting Mrs. Beaver in the face with a big red boot.

When Daisy pulled herself out of Little Pond, she saw that her explorer's hat drifted away, but grabbed it in time to not lose it forever. Her shirt and shorts were soaked and stained with mud. What an adventure already!

"I'm sorry to all of you, dear creatures!"

Daisy shouted to the fish, frogs, toads, beavers, turtles, birds, and bugs. A smile shined through her dirty face.

"I came looking for Science at your Little Pond after finding this map at my new house." Daisy held up a damp piece of paper in the air. "I brought along my book to help me make discoveries," she declared while she stood in one spot, drying off in the sun.

"You certainly did," said a voice near Daisy.

Gush, slosh, gurgle. Daisy's wet boots turned her around in a circle.

"Who said that?" she asked as she looked up into the blue sky, then down into the trees, along the long grass, and at Little Pond.

"Excuse me for not introducing myself before, but you appeared very, very busy. And if there is one thing I understand most, it is being very, very busy," stated Mrs. Beaver as she swam closer to shore. Beavers, by the way, can hold their breath much longer underwater than humans. Daisy knew this from her Science reading.

"Why, thank you," Daisy bowed. She didn't know why she bowed. It simply felt right. "My name is Daisy."

While Mrs. Beaver, who declared herself as Mrs. Beaver, chatted with her new human friend, a few more animals stopped by to listen. Out of the thick reeds came Snapper, the snapping turtle. Then followed Heron, the Great Blue Heron, Lady Canada Goose closely followed by her fellow, Lord Canada Goose, Murck and Muck the frogs, a Blue-fronted Dancer damselfly, and more! Daisy smiled in wonder and excitement.

Then, Mr. Beaver pulled himself away from his dam long enough to be polite and say 'hello'.

"Mr. Beaver, please use your manners and say 'hello' to Daisy, our visitor today," Mrs. Beaver suggested.

"Hello, visitor," Mr. Beaver said. "Welcome to our Little Pond."

"Why thank you, Mr. Beaver," Daisy laughed. "It's great of you to have me."

Finally, after all of the friendly *hellos* and *welcomes* were finished, Daisy asked a question.

"Am I the only human you have ever spoken to?" She placed a finger to her lip in thought.

"I think you are the first, at least for me," Mrs. Beaver smiled. "Anyone else?"

No one had an answer. The way the birds sang above her, and the frogs sat still at the edge of the water, to how gentle the dragonflies landed on the grass, Daisy felt there was something special about Little Pond. But as quickly as she arrived, sadly, suppertime neared, and Daisy left for home.

"Hope to see you tomorrow," she smiled and waved, then ran up the bank and out of sight.

Snapper turned to Mr. and Mrs. Beaver while Kingfisher flew over to join them.

"Hey, what's all the noise about here?" the bird asked.

"Noise?" Mr. Beaver raised his eyebrows. "You're the King of noise."

"Now, let's not argue," Mrs. Beaver said. "Hello, King. We were talking about a girl who came to our Little Pond. Her name is Daisy."

"A girl? What did she want?" King looked all around, head up and head down, ready to take flight.

"That's the thing," Snapper spoke up. "We aren't sure. But, she did say she was looking for something." Snapper stuck his foot to his mouth.

"The term you are looking for is Sigh Ence," Mrs. Beaver said very, very slowly. "Yes, that's the name of the what Daisy is searching for, but I have never heard of such a thing." Mrs. Beaver shook her head. King moved closer to Mr. Beaver, Mrs. Beaver, and Snapper. He spoke in a whisper.

"Sigh Ence? I have absolutely heard of Sigh Ence, and I can tell you, nothing good will come of it. I think our conversation must end right now!" And with this, King, the Kingfisher, flew away, rattling his voice as he did so.

11

Snapper huddled into his reeds. "What does that mean, Mrs. Beaver?"

"I'm not sure, but we must look into this. Daisy is friendly, but this Sigh Ence sounds, well, a bit scary," Mrs. Beaver declared.

"What is there to be afraid of? Who knows, maybe Sigh Ence is a nice fella? You know King. He is always screaming about something," Mr. Beaver comforted Snapper and Mrs. Beaver.

"I have an idea," Mrs.Beaver said."Why don't we gather the Little Pond Council and citizens to see if we can help Daisy find Sigh Ence. Then, when we do, we can leave Sigh Ence out for her near the pond tomorrow and this way she will..."

"Know we want to help her!" Snapper finished Mrs. Beaver's thought.

"Exactly!" Mrs.Beaver smiled.

The whole pond reflected the high sun. It was the perfect time for a gathering. Within a few minutes, all the animals of the Little Pond were called to a meeting at the Great Blue rock.

12

It was no coincidence this was where Heron, the Great Blue Heron, stayed during his naps. He stood upon his rock completely still, like a statue you see in a park or at a fountain.

"Hear ye! Hear ye! Calling all Council members and citizens of Little Pond!" Mr. Beaver sang out loud while waving a mighty branch that had hundreds of tiny acorns attached by willow strands.

Animals from within the pond swam to the rock, others hopped, flew, or walked to the edge closest to it. Even the citizens from the shade side of the pond made it to this unusual call for a meeting on a sunny summer Saturday.

The Little Pond Council, or Council, for short, was directed by frog brothers, Murck and Muck, both famous for their fairness. Then, Mr. and Mrs. Beaver held minor positions, as did Crow and Heron. They began the roll call of citizens immediately. As to not bore you for many, many minutes, here is a run-own of the citizens present:

Little Pond: all frogs and toads, fish, turtles, water-fowl (birds), non-waterfowl (birds, but not water-birds), chipmunks, spotted salamanders, insects (flying and nonflying), raccoons, skunks, deer, foxes, rabbits, and one Northern water snake.

The frogs called the meeting to order to calm the citizens and explain their purpose.

"We call this meeting official right now and will explain our purpose. We are here to calm all citizens of Little Pond by telling you our goal which is to honor the call for kindness on the behalf of all citizens," Murck began.

"It has been brought to our attention that a search party is requested on behalf of two members of our Council and one concerned citizen," Muck continued. "There is a human who needs our help finding..." here, Muck paused to ask Mrs. Beaver how to properly pronounce the name since she was now an expert, "Sigh Ence".

A murmur, or low grumbling of voices, rippled through the crowd.

"A mystery visitor, named Daisy, stopped by Little Pond today in the name of *Sigh Ence* for which she is hoping to discover here. Since we have never seen or heard of this item, whether animal or otherwise, we ask that you keep a lookout for what we do not know and what we have not seen, but out of the goodness of our hearts, we hope to find," Muck said. "We will meet here at sunrise tomorrow to see what you gather. Any questions?"

Mrs. Beaver, in her Council duty, recorded all questions in her memory and shared them with Mr. Beaver and Heron for them to keep in their memory to help the situation as much as possible. Here are the questions discussed:

King- Q: How do you know this human is safe?

Muck- A: We have eyewitness accounts she is harmless to animals.

Monarch- Q: She chased me all morning. What if she catches me?

Muck- A: Let her take your picture, and if she catches you, call us for help by screaming "Zebra!". It's our safe word.

Weasel- Q: I think I know Sigh Ence. She's slimy and lives down at the brook.

Muck- A: You're thinking of Slug, and she is harmless, I promise. A little gross, but no ill will there. Sigh Ence may not be an animal at all.

"Now, if all questions are answered, we send you on your way in the name of Sigh Ence!" Murck smiled. "Good will to you and good luck! Meeting Adjourned."

And that is how the Little Pond Council meeting with the citizens of Little Pond went on an early summer evening.

Snapper thought about helping Daisy while he searched for something, anything, he felt she needed. He never had a friend before, not knowing what one really was. Mr. and Mrs. Beaver were friends. They had to be. They were parents. Perhaps if Snapper helped her, he and Daisy would become friends.

The frogs were all friends, and the toads stuck together. The birds chose who they chatted with because some of them moved around during the seasons. The animals from the meadow kept close to be safe and for company on cold nights. Yet, none of this was true for Snapper. Life as a turtle was simple and lonely.

As for the other animals of Little Pond, all ears and eyes were open in the search for Sigh Ence. While the tiny Leopard Frog spoke to Lady Canada Goose, Snapper overheard him sharing his ideas.

"In my experience with situations like this," Leopard Frog said, "I think someone is hiding it right here at Little Pond!"

"You do not think so for sure?" asked Lady Canada Goose.

"Absolutely! Consider the last time we had a search party. We ended up sweeping dandelion seeds off of the reed puddles thinking they were magical snowflakes. And, whose bright idea was that?" Leopard Frog had his hand on his hips as he spoke and looked straight into Lady Canada Goose's eyes.

But Lady Canada Goose did not answer.

"Well, I will tell you. It was that Council, the same animals leading this newest adventure, and I, for one, decline my part," he said as he scampered away from Lady Canada Goose, his head held high in the air enough to think he was sniffing something delicious. But, that was Leopard Frog's way.

Meanwhile, Mr. and Mrs. Beaver collected some curious stones and sticks, their area of expertise, or great knowledge, and studied each one in careful detail.

"Mr. Beaver, I declare this is a piece of granite, native to our area, as you know," Mrs. Beaver said.

"It most certainly is, Mrs. Beaver" Mr. Beaver said. "Although this may not be Sigh Ence, I think it's worth bringing this fine pink specimen to the sunrise meeting." And together, Mr. and Mrs. Beaver headed back to their lodge for a snack.

The Little Pond animals had more energy than ever before! The frogs leapt and laughed among the lily pads, while the butterflies bounced around their Joe Pye Weed from head to head, gathering its sweet scent. The fish swam in tiny schools, circling small rocks at the pond's edges, and Skunk ran with his children into the blackberry brambles.

For the rest of his evening, Snapper swam and then walked from rock to rock and log to log, looking low and looking high for anything worthy of the Sunrise Meeting. As he was about to head home without anything, Snapper found one precious item to bring. Above the reeds stood a tall and fat bush filled with green leaves and berries that reminded him of fish eggs. The original seeds made their way down the brook and to Little Pond many, many years ago. Of course, Snapper did not know this, but he felt it was special for a reason he could not explain, a sort of magical quality to it.

When the stars came out, the diurnals (animals active during the day) prepared for sleep, and the nocturnals (animals active at night) began their search. Raccoon gathered her two sons to pick through

a variety of rubbish she had collected and stored in their hollow oak, anything ranging from a broken toilet seat to a small orange vase. Although Raccoon did not know what these objects were named or used for, she felt they may be important one day.

The Big Brown Bat raced from his forest home and flew above Little Pond, excited at the news of something unusual.

While he dove after beetles back and forth above Mr. and

Mrs. Beaver's lodge, he saw Mrs. Beaver begin her night's work with a bit more enthusiasm, or enjoyment, than usual.

"Hello Big Brown Bat," she called above. "Have you heard the news?"

"Yes," Big Brown Bat yelled below. "It's very exciting. I'm sure to find a sign of Sigh Ence in my travels. I will drop off anything I find to you on your house, next to Lady Canada Goose's nest, since I will be going home to sleep at sunrise."

"A perfect plan!" Mrs. Beaver yelled back. As the moon rose higher in the night sky, the animals of Little Pond looked at the stars in wonder, for their lives were about to change in ways they did not yet know.

At dawn, when Big Brown Bat, Raccoon, and the nocturnal animals returned to their homes to rest, Mrs. Beaver decided to put aside her normal nap time to help Mr. Beaver with the Sunrise Meeting.

By the time Mr. Beaver and Mrs. Beaver arrived at Heron's rock, the morning was warm and an excitement filled the air! From Snapper's reeds, he watched animals come from all directions, each carrying pieces of something or other in the name of Sigh Ence. Murk and Muck called all to order.

"We officially call to order the Sunrise Meeting," Murck began.

Snapper looked at the citizens of Little Pond, and they all looked at each other. Smiles grew, and even some chuckles escaped as they shared their discoveries.

"Let us begin setting up our items together to see what sense we can make of what you have found," Muck suggested. "Mr. and Mrs. Beaver have generously donated small logs to wall off our exhibit, meaning an area where you display items for others to look at. Thank you to the Beaver family."

For a few moments, the animals simply stood there, not knowing how to begin. Of course, this was the perfect opportunity for someone who was used to giving orders to help direct the display of Sigh Ence items. Mr. Beaver stepped forward.

"May I suggest to the Council organizing the display by size?" Mr. Beaver asked.

"I'm not sure what that means, but I think it sounds perfectly fine," Muck responded. "Do you think so, Murck?"

"Absolutely," Murck said to Muck. "If Mr. Beaver has a great idea, then let the display begin!"

To this, the animals moved forward in a single file line, and Mrs. Beaver directed them to Mr. Beaver, who then examined each piece of evidence for the exhibit of Sigh Ence.

Some of the pieces the animals found were no bigger than an acorn, while others, like the granite, were a bit larger. Each one was a different shape, color, and size. It looked like Sigh Ence lived everywhere!

The morning flew by when Crow cawed from the top of his hemlock.

"Caw! Caw! Here comes the Daisy!" he shouted.

"Someone must distract her," Snapper spoke loud enough to surprise himself. "We have to finish in the name of Sigh Ence!"

"Leave it to me," said Monarch. "I can handle it!" The lovely orange and black Monarch sped away into the green forest.

Meanwhile, Mr. Beaver, breathless with work, gathered the Council and Snapper to the exhibit.

"Do you think we have everything?" he asked while wiping sweat off his furry face. He looked at Heron, Snapper, and Pileated Woodpecker, a new member of the Council since that moment.

"I brought a piece of what is called a 'fence' from the old house I like to visit on days when I need a pick me up of carpenter ants," Pileated Woodpecker said. "I know it as such because the human who lives there shakes his hand in the air and says, 'Hey bird! Get off my fence!'. I thought that since fence makes an 'ence' sound, it can be part of what we're searching for!" He then puffed out his black and white chest feathers.

"How exciting" said Snapper.

Suddenly, Crow cawed once more. "She's headed this way!"

Muck and Murck lead the animals away from the exhibit.

"Citizens of Little Pond, the Council thanks you for your hard work. Now, let us see if Daisy finds Sigh Ence in our exhibit."

"That Monarch is fast," said Daisy. "How nice of her to stop on a flower and let me take a picture."

24

As she rounded the grassy corner where the wildflowers end and the reeds begin, Daisy nearly ran into the official Sigh Ence display! At first, her mouth opened, but no words came out. Then, she placed her hand on her heart and said

"Oh my, my, my!"

She bent over to investigate the exhibit closely. Flowers, rocks, seeds, an orange vase, dried beetles, leaves, fishing line, a piece of old bread, the 'ence' of a fence, still spiders, and more. In the middle of it all was Snapper's branch of fish egg berries.

"This is amazing!" Daisy gasped. "In the name of Science, everything here must be brought home and looked at closely. But, I wonder *how it got here.*"

Suddenly, a great gust of wind blew, and dark clouds filled the sky. Then, it began to rain.

"Our Sigh Ence!" Heron cried. He flew from his rock, landed next to the exhibit, and spread his giant wings over it.

All of the Little Pond animals came out into the rain, while Daisy took cover under the old oak. One by one, the citizens took their Sigh Ence discoveries to Daisy.

"Wow! All of you are my little scientists!" she laughed. "Thank you, thank you, thank you!" She turned to Heron, soaking wet in his hurry to help. "And thanks to you, Heron, for being my hero today. Without you, all of this would be soaked and hard to bring home."

Heron bowed his beak and placed a wing over his red face.

"Good thing I brought a basket to collect berries." Daisy began to fill her basket with Sigh Ence as the animals watched in excitement. Then, the rain fell away and a rainbow appeared in the sky. "It appears I'm not the only one who loves to explore nature." Daisy leaned over to Heron and Mrs. Beaver. "If you see, my Science book has animals, water, rocks, everything! I think you covered it all. I have a whole summer of fun in my basket."

Daisy made herself a place on the grass and nibbled on wild blueberries, looking all around and smiling. Then Dancer, the Blue-fronted Damselfly, landed on her shorts and looked up at her.

"Why hello, Dancer! Would you like to see what is in my basket?"

Dancer crisscrossed upwards as Daisy reached into her basket and pulled out Snapper's branch.

"Do you see this? It's called Autumn Olive. If you read my Science book with me, you know it is called an invasive species, which means it does not belong at your pond. I will make sure to help you clean it up over the summer. Good thing we found it before it keeps your flowers from growing!"

Snapper's heart grew while he listened. His contribution for Daisy did mean something after all!

Suddenly, Daisy sat up straight and looked right at Snapper. "Little snapping turtle," she asked, "did you find this branch? If so, thank *you*."

She looked at each item and matched them with the animal who found it.

"Mr. and Mrs. Beaver? Is this a piece of granite? That's awesome!"

"Did you hear her?" Mr. Beaver asked Mrs. Beaver. "She said I'm awesome."

"Yeah, well, she needs to get to know you," Mrs. Beaver said.

Daisy then came to the shore, her boots hitting the water.

"Thank you for all of your hard work, animals! Thank you for welcoming me to your Little Pond. This is the perfect place to explore!" She clapped her hands together in happiness.

"Feel free to bring a lunch and share," said Snapper with all the courage he had in him.

"I will, I will, I promise, my friends!" Daisy said as she picked up her full basket of Sigh Ence, waved goodbye for the day, and headed home before dark.

"Friends," she said to herself and clapped quietly. "I have friends."

"Friends," Snapper said to himself on his way back to the reeds. "We are friends."

After an exciting adventure, life returned to almost normal at Little Pond, but the animals knew it never would be the same. Snapper sunk into his reeds, the birds flew into trees, the frogs and fish all went home. Mr. and Mrs. Beaver swam by their lodge, blending into the brown. All was quiet, as was Heron on his rock, pretending to nap, the happiest animal of them all for he became a hero that day.

DAISY'S FIELD NOTES-

At our new house, I found a map, and I headed out to find Little Pond! In the name of Science, I declare to discover all I can about it, my new favorite place in the world. The best part, I made friends. Tomorrow, I continue to explore.

Discovered Today -

1 Monarch, 2 frogs, 1 crow, 1 very noisy Kingfisher, 2 beavers and their babies, 1 turtle, 2 geese, 1 heron, 1 damselfly, and many, many friends.

Explorer's Final Words

Science and discoveries are everywhere! The treasures given to me today can be used in the name of Science. It's all thanks to my dear friends at Little Pond. For the love of nature, I plan to return the favor soon!

The End

Shennen Flannery loves teaching high school English and living in the Northwest corner of Connecticut with her amazing family.

In addition to her two wonderful children, Alden and Alice, and her supportive husband, Brian, she has three very busy rescued mutts and a horse, Annie, who lives down the road.

The love of nature surrounds her home and provides endless inspiration for stories! Shennen has been writing since childhood and uses stories as a springboard to express emotions for children and teens who may struggle most in this area of life. She earned her degree in English and Writing from Central Connecticut University, then a Master's in Education from Plymouth State University, and recently completed McDaniel College's graduate program of Writing for children and young adults.

When she is not teaching or writing, Shennen is outdoors walking her most antiquated canine and soul mate, Sunny, or gardening among her flowers spread haphazardly throughout her property.

Made in the USA
Middletown, DE
29 May 2020